When You Take a Pig to a Party

by Kristina Thermaenius McLarey & Myra McLarey

pictures by Marjory Wunsch

ORCHARD BOOKS • NEW YORK

Thanks to Elena Castedo and The Porch Table — M.M. AND M.W.

Text copyright © 2000 by Kristina Thermaenius McLarey and Myra McLarey
Illustrations copyright © 2000 by Marjory Wunsch

Orchard Books, A Grolier Company, 95 Madison Avenue, New York, NY 10016

Manufactured in the United States of America
Printed and bound by Phoenix Color Corp. Book design by Mina Greenstein
The text of this book is set in 14 point Meridien. The illustrations are gouache.

1 3 5 7 9 10 8 6 4 2

Library of Congress Cataloging-in-Publication Data
McLarey, Kristina Thermaenius.
When you take a pig to a party / Kristina Thermaenius McLarey and Myra McLarey ;
illustrated by Marjory Wunsch.   p.   cm.
Summary: Havoc ensues when Adelaide takes her usually well-behaved pet pig to a friend's
birthday party.
ISBN 0-531-30257-1 (trade : alk. paper).—ISBN 0-531-33257-8 (lib. bdg. : alk. paper)
[1. Pigs Fiction. 2. Parties Fiction. 3. Humorous stories.]
I. McLarey, Myra, date. II. Wunsch, Marjory, ill. III. Title.
PZ7.M4786975Wh 2000 [E]—dc21 99-36897

For Amilia
—K.T.M. AND M.M.

To Ruth, Toli, Helen, and Harry
—M.W.

This little girl is Adelaide, and the pig beside her is Sherman.

Adelaide and Sherman do lots of things together. They swing on the tire swing hanging from the black oak tree. They slide down the hay pile in the barn. And they like a good game of horseshoes after supper.

Adelaide has always said that Sherman is the dearest, sweetest, most wonderful, and best-behaved pig in the world.

So, of course, she thought it would be okay to take him to Ethan's birthday party—especially since she gave Sherman a bath, sprinkled some of her mother's best perfume on him, and tied her father's polka-dot bow tie around his neck.

Things did go just dandy at first. Sherman loved musical chairs and even won pin-the-tail-on-the-donkey. But then Adelaide got so carried away watching Marlon the Magician that she forgot to keep an eye on Sherman.

So before she knew it, Sherman was in the flower garden munching away. And when Ethan's daddy saw Sherman, he bellowed, "THERE'S A PIG IN OUR PEONIES!"

And Adelaide and Ethan and all of the children took off after Sherman, yelling, "STOP, SHERMAN, STOP!"

But Sherman, thinking that they wanted to play chase, started running in circles and bumped into Ethan's daddy, sending popcorn *ker-swirling* like a January blizzard.

Which startled Sherman, who ran between Marlon the Magician's legs, causing the rabbit just popping out of Marlon's hat to land *ker-plop* on Sherman's back.

Which astonished Sherman so much that he scampered through a hole under the fence to where the McKinneys were having a barbecue.

In fact, Sherman was running so fast he didn't even see the McKinneys' swimming pool until he landed *ker-splat* right in it.

And the McKinneys and all their guests roared, "THERE'S A PIG IN THE POOL!" And Adelaide and Ethan and all of the children chased after Sherman, hollering, "STOP, SHERMAN, STOP!" But Sherman didn't stop. Instead he *ker-splashed* across the pool, scrambled out, and squeezed through a loose plank into Mrs. Primrose's yard.

And before Adelaide could get a word out, Sherman was heading through the open door into Mrs. Primrose's house, where she was hosting a bridge-club luncheon. "EEK! THERE'S A PIG IN MY PARLOR!" shrieked Mrs. Primrose. Whereupon, Cassandra, Mrs. Primrose's cat—so dismayed to see a pig in her house—took a flying leap and landed *ker-blunk* on Sherman's back.

And Adelaide and Ethan and all of the children—with muddy clothes and muddy feet—tramped through Mrs. Primrose's parlor, crying, "STOP, SHERMAN, STOP!"

But Sherman was already in the next yard, where Mrs. Hayden was painting her flower boxes. And when Mr. Hayden stuck his head out of the window to see what the commotion was all about, he tipped a pot of geraniums into a bucket of paint, sending paint *ker-splattering*—over everything and everybody.

Mrs. Hayden squealed, "THERE'S A PIG IN OUR PAINT!" And Adelaide and Ethan and all of the children—with muddy clothes and muddy feet and paint in their hair and on their best party clothes—shouted, "STOP, SHERMAN, STOP!"

But Sherman simply would not stop.

Instead he darted across the street, where Mr. Whipple was watering his lawn. And when Mr. Whipple turned in surprise, he sprayed water all over Mr. and Mrs. Rice, who were just coming home from the bakery. And that, of course, caused them to throw up their hands in despair, sending doughnuts *ker-plunking, ker-crumbling* all over the sidewalk.

Adelaide and Ethan and all of the children scurried over Mr. Whipple's lawn, screaming, "STOP, SHERMAN, STOP!"

And finally, at long last, Sherman stopped.

To eat the doughnuts, of course.

But just as Adelaide was about to grab Sherman by his bow tie,

Mr. and Mrs. Rice howled, "THERE'S A PIG IN OUR PASTRY!"

Which gave Sherman such a fright he took off again, heading straight for Lucy Marple, who was coming down the street on her brand-new skateboard.

"HELP, THERE'S A PIG IN MY PATH!" Lucy hollered. Adelaide and Ethan and all of the children called out at the top of their lungs, "JUMP, LUCY! JUMP OFF!"

But when Lucy jumped off her skateboard, it did a backward flip and landed *ker-plunk* under Sherman's feet.

Which sent Sherman careening toward Ethan's yard, where Ethan's mother was putting the candles on the prettiest, yummiest, most delicious, most scrumptious-looking birthday cake you ever saw.

And Adelaide and Ethan and all of the children wailed, "OH NO, NOT THE CAKE!"

And they yelled and hollered and screamed and shrieked and cried and shouted and begged, "STOP, SHERMAN, PLEASE STOP!"

And *ker-smack*, *ker-bash*, *ker-boom!* He did.

So if you ask Adelaide, she'll tell you,
"You never know what will happen when you
take a pig to a party!"

Especially if his name is Sherman.

The Duck Says

Troy Wilson

illustrated by
Mike Boldt

SCHOLASTIC INC.

ISBN 978-1-338-03466-0

12 11 10 9 8 7 6 5 4 3 2   16 17 18 19 20 21

Printed in the U.S.A.   40

This edition first printing, January 2016

To Poet Ter (aka Terry Gilbert Morris) and
Nana (aka Vivian Deer Richmond).
— T. W.

To Seth and Jonas, who have endless questions
and things to say.
— M. B.

The duck says **Quack!**

2

or when he gets chased
by a big swarm of bees.

The duck says

Duck!

so you won't get hit.

6

The duck says

Goose!

when he means that you're it.

The duck says

Ooops!

when he makes a mistake.

10

The duck says

Waaah!

when he cries like a baby.

The duck says

Hmmm ...

when he's thinking
"Just maybe ..."

The duck says **Whoa!** when he's riding a horse.

Unless he just wants
to keep going, of course.

The duck says **Honk!**

to a bunch of slow drakes.

The duck says

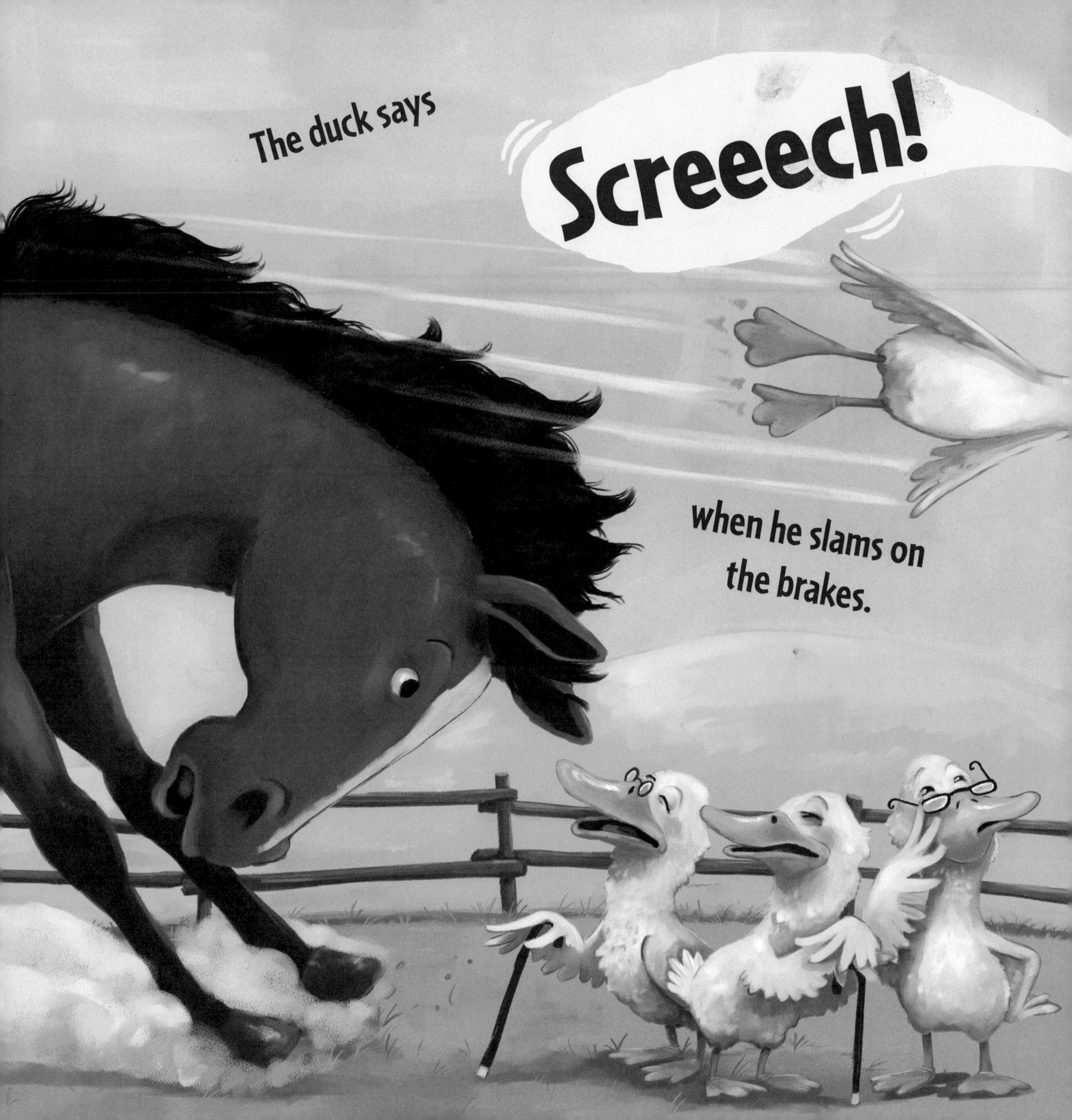

when he slams on the brakes.

The duck says

Shh...

when the bees are too near.

The duck says

Phew!

when the coast
is all clear.

19

The duck says

Oink!

when he eats like a pig.

20

The duck says

Snore.

when he falls really deep.

23

The duck says

Ahh . . .

when he opens
his eyes.

The duck says WHAAAT?! to express his surprise.

The duck says

Darn!

because then he
forgets it.

The duck says

The . . .

as he rushes on by.

The duck says

End.

and I think you know why.

Stella's STARS

Jane Edgecombe

Illustrated by Helen Brawley

Stella was an only child. She missed her Mom and Dad. They'd gone away to Mandalay, and left her feeling sad.
Mandalay was far away. She couldn't go, they'd said. They wanted her to stay behind and go to school instead.
They promised they would write. Then after hugging one another,
They'd packed poor Stella off to go and live with her Grandmother!

Her Grandma's
house was big
and old, and full of funny things,
Like stuffed fruit bats, and
paper lamps, and pirate
ships on strings.
Her Grandma said 'You're free to play
with anything you like –
The walking fish, the wedding
dress, the penny-farthing bike –
There's only one thing in this house
that you must never touch,
And that's my golden music box.
I treasure it too much!'

That afternoon, her Grandmother went
out to buy some prunes,
And Stella found the music box, all carved
with stars and moons.
She opened it a crack, and heard a tinkling
silver bell,
And she saw a golden bracelet lying there
inside as well.
She thought she'd try it on her wrist,
and noticed as she did,
Some writing carved inside the
golden music box's lid.
'The bracelet takes you far away,
five stars will bring you back'
'Uh, oh,' she thought, 'I've done
it now!'
And Stella's world
went black.

She was sucked
into the music box
and out the other side,
Where she splashed
into a starry sea as
deep as it was wide.
Above her stars were
twinkling, and below her starfish, too,
Seemed to wave at her with all their
starry arms of brightest hues.
She stretched out on her back into a star
shape, so she'd float.
Which is always the best thing to do if you
forget your boat.
The current gently washed her to a
wizard in a cave,
Who gave to her a little golden star for being
very brave.

'Young girl,' he said,
'you'll need to find four
more to get you home.
I think by far the
best way is to ask a
passing gnome.'
He pointed to the
darkness of the gloomy caves beyond,
Then vanished as a cloud of smoke puffed
from his starry wand.
Stella stumbled forward, and at once she
bumped her knee
'Watch out!' said a little gnome, 'You've
bumped right into me!'
'I'm sorry!' Stella said. 'But it's so very
dark in here!'
The gnome gave her a glowing star
'This might help, my dear.'

By her little bit of
starlight Stella walked on till
she found,
An enormous twinkling cavern
far beneath the stony ground,
Where a flock of fiery dragons
flapped their green and golden
wings,
Round a mound of brightest gems and
gold – a treasure fit for kings.
But Stella saw a naughty gnome
amongst the treasure, trying
To throw gems at a little
one who wasn't good at flying!
'Stop that!' Stella cried. 'Thanks
child!' the little dragon hissed,
And with her teeth she
gently put a star on Stella's wrist.

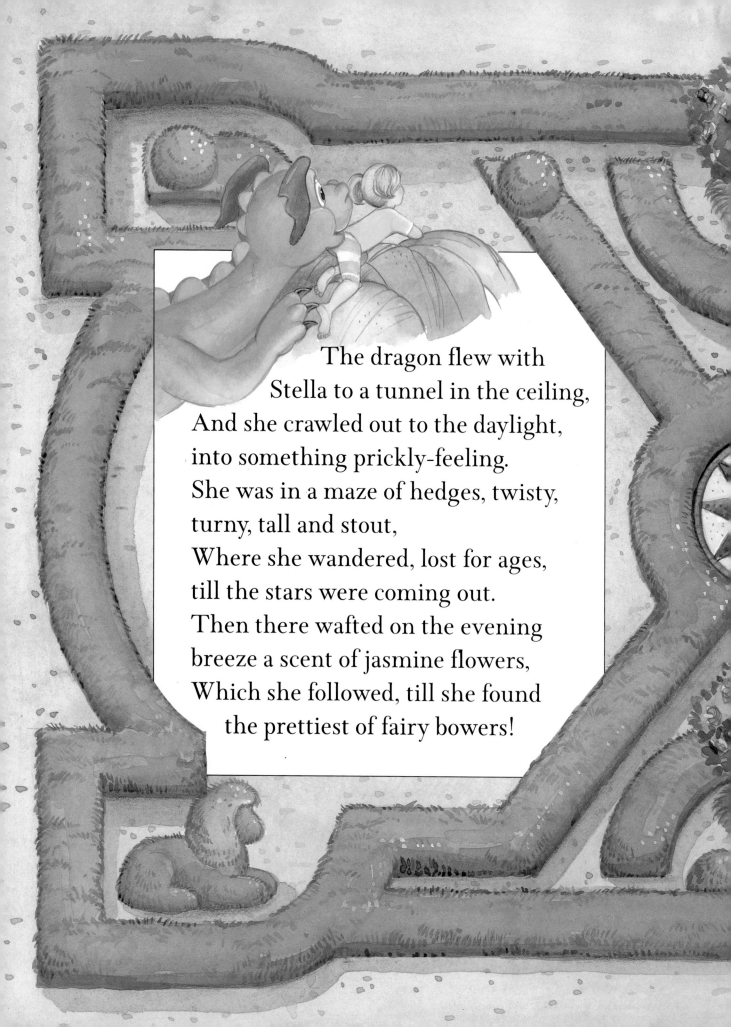

The dragon flew with
Stella to a tunnel in the ceiling,
And she crawled out to the daylight,
into something prickly-feeling.
She was in a maze of hedges, twisty,
turny, tall and stout,
Where she wandered, lost for ages,
till the stars were coming out.
Then there wafted on the evening
breeze a scent of jasmine flowers,
Which she followed, till she found
the prettiest of fairy bowers!

She plucked a little star shaped
flower to enjoy the scent,
It magically turned golden, and
onto her bracelet went!
She was going to pick another, but the
flowers moved aside
To reveal the Fairy Queen. A silver box was
by her side.
'Don't you know your name
means star?' she said,
'just look in here.'
In the box there was
a mirror, showing Stella's
face so clear.
The mirror Stella handed to her other self a star.
'Oh thankyou!' Stella said, ' and what a pretty girl
you are!'
Now Stella had five stars,
The Music box began to chime.
It called Stella back to Grandma's house,
Just in the nick   of time.

She zapped back out
the music box, and
quickly closed the lid.
Her Grandmother
walked in and said
'Hello dear!' as she did.
'It's fun here, Grandma!' Stella said, 'I'm glad I
live with you!'
Her Grandma patted Stella's arm and said 'I'm
so glad too.'
Her Grandma touched the bracelet.
  Stella's heart began to sink.
  'I've got one exactly like that!' said
    her Grandma, with a wink.